D0795111

Puffin Books
Editor: Kaye Webb
The Elephant Party *and other stories*

'A great big pink elephant. A wibbly wobbly elephant. A shivery shaky elephant . . . fatter than fat.' A circus elephant which gave the children the best party they had ever had. This is only one of the pleasing and puzzling creatures which appear in these new stories by a master of modern fairy tales. A timid starling gets to Africa ahead of all his fellows – but without a single wing-beat; rude squirrels force a mole, a mouse and a hedgehog to leave their comfortable home, but they find a new one, and a magic teapot to go with it; a rocking horse has to learn that his place is in the nursery; a witch's stolen shoes take their revenge on a cheeky boy, and a misunderstood giant makes friends with a village of 'stuck-up' people.

There are even more surprises to come in this comical, magical, animal, vegetable, mineral collection of stories for readers of four and over, all told with a gaiety which creates a warm feeling of happiness for children who listen and adults who read to them.

Paul Biegel

The Elephant Party

and other stories

Translated from the Dutch by Patricia Crampton
Illustrated by Babs van Wely

Puffin Books

Puffin Books, Penguin Books Ltd, Harmondsworth, Middlesex, England
Penguin Books, 625 Madison Avenue, New York, New York 10022, U.S.A.
Penguin Books Australia Ltd, Ringwood, Victoria, Australia
Penguin Books Canada Ltd, 2801 John Street, Markham, Ontario,
Canada L3R 1B4
Penguin Books (N.Z.) Ltd, 182–190 Wairau Road, Auckland 10, New Zealand

First published in Holland by Uitgeversmaatschappij Holland – Haarlem, 1973
under the title *Het Olifantenfeest*
Published in Puffin Books 1977
First published in Great Britain 1977

Made and printed in Great Britain by
Richard Clay (The Chaucer Press) Ltd,
Bungay, Suffolk
Set in Monotype Bembo

Contents

The Elephant Party

The circus was coming! All the cars had to stop, and no one was allowed to cross the road any more, because the circus would be coming right down the middle of the street.

'Tarantara!' Twelve men tooted the music on their copper oompah-pas, which glittered in the sunshine.

'Boom! Boom! Boom!' The big drum followed behind. It was almost impossible to see the man who was beating the big drum, because the drum was ten times as big as his tummy.

And the clowns! They did not walk, they ran and skipped and danced and hopped and pulled funny faces at Mrs Keepoff de Grasse.

Behind the clowns walked the lion-tamer, with two savage lions, but they were firmly attached to a chain and walked along as demurely as puppy-dogs.

There were horses, too, and caravan after caravan after caravan. The parade took at least an hour to pass by.

'Hurrah!' cried all the children in the street. 'Hurrah for the circus!'

'But there aren't any elephants,' cried a little girl. She was very fond of elephants.

'There! There!' shouted her little brother. 'There's one coming now!'

And lo and behold, right at the back, last of all in the long procession, came a great big grey jumbo. But how oddly he moved! So jerkily, so flabbily, so . . . so . . .

Then all the children shouted: 'It's not real! It's not a real elephant! It's an elephant on wheels!'

They had never seen anything so funny. An elephant which looked like a toy elephant, but was as big as a real one! What could it mean? The procession stopped in the middle of the square, the caravans forming a big circle. The tent was put up and the elephant came to a stop beside it. The children were allowed to come quite close. He was big, he was very big!

'Ladies and Gentlemen!' cried the ringmaster of the circus, who was wearing a tall hat. 'Ladies and Gentlemen, this elephant is a very remarkable beast. If you will all help, you will find out just how remarkable it is. Will you all help?'

'Yeees!' shouted everybody, for everybody had come to look. There must have been about a thousand people in the square.

'Listen!' said the ringmaster. 'All the mothers must go home and cook a big saucepan of pudding – pink pudding,

8

raspberry pudding. And when the puddings are ready, all the mothers must come back here, to the elephant. With the saucepans of pudding.'

'And then?' asked the thousand people.

'You will see!' cried the ringmaster. And then he said something absolutely horrible. He said: 'All the children must go to bed!'

'Heeey!' shouted all the children.

'Otherwise the party can't go on,' said the ringmaster. 'The elephant party. It begins tomorrow morning. All the children can come then.'

There was nothing else for it: the children were packed off to bed. Their mothers began to cook puddings which you could smell all over town. Raspberry puddings. They smelled pink.

After an hour people began to arrive from all sides, mothers with steaming hot pans, and fathers too, because there are a great many fathers who can cook, and aunts and grandmothers and even kind ladies who had no children at all. Every one of them had a great pan, full of hot pudding.

'This way!' called the ringmaster.

Two ladders were propped against the elephant. By each ladder stood a clown and the clowns took the pans of pudding, climbed the ladder with them and poured them out . . . into the elephant.

There was an opening in the top of the elephant, and it

was getting fuller and fuller. In the end, when the last pan of pudding had been handed up by a nervous grandmother and poured out, the elephant was stuffed – stuffed with raspberry pudding.

'Now isn't that a shame!' said the people.

'Wait a bit!' said the ringmaster. 'At eight o'clock tomorrow morning all the children – *all* the children – must come here. With a spoon!'

That was more like it! By seven o'clock they were already lined up: Charlie and Jock and Hannah and Gerry and Mike and the doctor's Till and a thousand more children, every one of them with a spoon. Some with soup spoons and one child with the biggest ladle in the kitchen.

'Where's the pudding gone?' they asked.

10

The grown-ups hadn't given anything away.

'Tarantara!' There was the music, and here came the clowns! And what did the clowns do? They began to peel the skin off the elephant. Rip, rip! And what was left after that?

A great big pink elephant. A wibbly wobbly elephant. A shivery shaky elephant. A pudding elephant, with a pudding tail and a pudding head and pudding feet, fatter than fat, and a pudding tum, rounder than round, oh yes, the most enormous pudding in the world. Pink, with a white cap of whipped cream on its head.

'Oooh!' shouted all the children and then the elephant party began. Ladders were run up against the pudding creature, at least ten of them, and at once the biggest boys and girls climbed up them, spoon in hand, and began to eat. From its back, from its neck, from its head, from its whipped cream cap. Smaller children began at the sides and the smallest of all at the feet. Pudding, pudding and more pudding they ate, with big spoons, little spoons, teaspoons, sauce spoons and one little boy with his ladle. They ate pink raspberry pudding at eight o'clock in the morning and the whole day long. The whole day, because the elephant was so big, so very big. When the real circus began that evening in the tent, the elephant had gone. All gone.

And all the children had fat, round tummies, as fat as the music man's big drum.

The Magic Trumpet

Bart had a grandfather and Grandfather had a trumpet. It hung on the wall, so high that Bart couldn't reach it, and it shone like gold.

'It's a magic trumpet,' said his grandfather. 'When you blow on it once, the old soldier comes. When you blow on it twice, the fairy comes, but when you blow on it three times the wicked wolf comes.'

'Won't you do it, Grandfather?' asked Bart.

'Another time, my boy.'

That was what Grandfather always said: another time. When would that be? Or wasn't it a magic trumpet at all?

'Grandfather,' asked Bart, 'have you ever blown on it *once*?'

'To be sure I have, my boy. What did you think?'

'And what did the old soldier look like?'

'Ah, my boy, he walked with a stoop and his coat hung down to the ground. And his gun was rusty.'

'And what did he do, Grandfather?'

'What did he do, my boy? I'll tell you. He asked for a pipe of tobacco.'

'Oh,' said Bart. 'Was he coming from the wars?'

'Yes, my boy. From a war in the past. It's so long ago, we don't want to think about it any more.'

'No,' said Bart. 'And Grandfather, have you ever blown on it *twice*?'

'To be sure I have, my boy. What did you think?'

'And what did the fairy look like?'

'Ah, my boy, the fairy wore a veil and a golden crown and she had a wand in her hand which gave off sparks. She could grant wishes with it.'

'With her wand, Grandfather?'

'Yes, my boy.'

'Did she make anything for you by magic, Grandfather?'

'Oh, my boy, I'm an old man. I no longer have any wishes.'

'But you could ask for some coloured chalks,' said Bart, 'and a racetrack with model cars. I would ask for a hundred and eight thousand and five model cars. And a bicycle. A racing bicycle, Grandfather. And chewing-gum and a cake and . . .'

'Stop, stop, my boy!' Grandfather put his fingers in his ears. 'I'm sure the fairy wouldn't like that at all.'

'Well then, just one model car, a little one. Oh please, Grandfather, couldn't I have a blow?'

'Are you cracked, my boy? Just imagine if it went wrong. Imagine if you blew three times, by mistake!'

Bart was startled. 'Would the wicked wolf really come then?' he asked.

'Of course it would really come!' cried Grandfather. 'What did you think?'

'Grandfather,' whispered Bart, 'have you ever blown on it *three* times?'

'Yes, my boy, I have,' said Grandfather with a sigh.

'And what did the wicked wolf look like?'

'Ah, my boy, the wicked wolf has a grey coat and a furry tail and he howls like the wind.'

Then Bart had to go home and next Sunday he could not visit his grandfather, because his grandfather was ill. Quite seriously ill, his mother said.

So ill that his mother went to see him in the middle of the week. Bart couldn't stay at home alone, so he went too. But he was not allowed to go to Grandfather's bedside. He had to wait down in the sitting-room like a good boy. In the sitting-room, where the trumpet was hanging.

Like a good boy.

But Bart pushed a chair against the wall, climbed on to it and took the trumpet down from its hook.

'I'm going to blow twice,' he thought, 'and then I shall ask the fairy to make Grandfather better.'

Would she really come?

Bart was trembling like a little boy, but of course he was

a big boy. He put the trumpet to his mouth and blew very cautiously.

Not a sound came out.

He blew harder. 'Hoooup!' it went suddenly.

Once.

Bart dropped the trumpet in a fright. Once, that meant that the old soldier would come with his rusty gun.

But nothing happened. 'Perhaps he's already dead,' thought Bart.

He picked up the trumpet. He knew how to do it now. He blew out his cheeks: 'Hoooup! Hoooup!' Two short blasts echoed round the room.

Nothing happened.

'Fairy!' called Bart softly.

But no one appeared, and suddenly Bart was dreadfully

angry. Grandfather had made a fool of him. It was not a magic trumpet. He took a deep breath and blew three mighty blasts on the trumpet. You see? Not a wicked wolf in sight. The room was still empty. Only Bart's mother came in. 'You can come and see Grandfather now,' she said.

Grandfather was propped up in bed, smiling a little. 'I heard you blowing, my boy.'

Bart turned red right up to the ears.

'You can have the trumpet now,' said Grandfather. 'It's for you.'

'But it isn't a magic trumpet at all,' said Bart.

'Oh, but it is, my boy,' said Grandfather. 'Have a look in that chest; there's an old coat in it and a rusty gun, because I myself am the old soldier. And the fairy is your mother; she wore a white veil when she married and she gives you everything you need, and, as for the wicked wolf, my boy, you will never have to be afraid of him. He only comes when you're an old grandfather, like me. And old grandfathers are not afraid.'

So Bart was given the magic trumpet, which was not really a magic trumpet. Or only a little bit.

The Timid Starling

Starlings are noisy creatures. When a dozen of them sit in a tree, they sound like at least a hundred. They whistle and scream and croak all at the same time, until suddenly they take flight and go and land on another tree, where they find still more friends. Or they all fly up out of the trees at the same time; then there are at least a hundred or a thousand of them and it looks as if a dark cloud were sweeping across the sky. A crazy cloud, a magic cloud, which changes into a giant or an old woman or a billowing sea.

But Klee never wanted to join in. Klee was a timid starling who always hid himself away. He sat in nooks and crannies and never dared to join his screaming friends or fly with them in the magic cloud.

'Klee's a cowardy custard,' they said, and, once they had said it, Klee was not even allowed to join in any more.

He didn't think that was too bad, but later, in the autumn, he thought it was very bad indeed, for it was then that the other starlings told him: 'You can't migrate with us, either.'

Migrate. That meant make the great journey which the birds make before winter to the hot countries. They fly over oceans and mountains and forests until they have caught up with the summer weather, for they fly south when it is winter here.

'You stay here in your cranny,' the starlings told Klee, 'on your own. You are always on your own, after all.'

Klee was upset, but he said: 'Then I shall fly south on my own as well.'

'Ha ha!' cried the others. 'You can't do that. You don't know the way on your own and you will get tired much too quickly. You hardly ever fly.'

And one shouted: 'I bet you don't even know how!'

But Klee did know how to fly. Next morning, when all the other starlings had moved off with a lot of noise, he came out, took a last good look round for safety's sake, stretched out his wings and climbed towards the blue sky. He felt so fine and free, he looped the loop, let himself drop like a stone, soared up again just in time and swooped down on a rowan tree. He ate one or two of the red bobbles and then he said: 'Now I shall journey to the south.' It sounded like a lonely starling-cheep.

He flew and he flew and he flew. Straight on, but now and then a little bit to the left and a little bit to the right. He flew over cities and forests and rivers. The cities were noisy, the forests were autumn gold and the rivers were like wriggling snakes.

But the south lay far away. However hard he peered, Klee could not see the summer anywhere. 'Oof,' he said, landing on a tall fence, 'oof'.

When it was dark, Klee felt very much alone. 'I'm lost,' he thought. 'I shall never find the way.' And he was tired. 'If only I had a cosy nook,' he thought, 'I would stay in it all winter. I don't care any more.'

He was a sad starling. And he was hungry.

Then Klee saw a little light in the distance. It was a house, a fine house with a crust of bread on the garden path and crumbs just under the window. Klee gobbled them up at once. Perhaps there would be still more on the window-sill. He was so hungry that he became a bold starling and sat right in front of the open window. But there was no bread on the window-sill. Instead, there was something else. A cosy nook.

A safe, dark nook, just the right size for a starling. Klee did not stop to think. He hopped towards it, jumped in, crept into the deepest corner, yawned an enormous yawn and fell asleep.

Klee's friends were by then already well on their way to the south. But birds are not the only things which fly that way.

People do too. In aeroplanes. And at the controls of an aeroplane sits a pilot. He is a man in a blue coat, and he wears a cap, a cap with a peak and a high front. So high that there is quite a nook inside it. The pilot of the aeroplane which was due to fly south that night had left home late. He had put his jacket on quickly, snatched up his cap from the window-sill and driven quickly to the airfield. So quickly that he did not notice how heavy his cap had become. As if there were something inside it. He didn't even notice as he raced towards the aeroplane to be in time, and once he was in the air he was too busy with all the little lights and dials. The aeroplane flew south in one night, high above all the birds flying in the same direction.

Not until the aeroplane had landed again, and the pilot got out after all the other people, did he think of his cap. 'Oof,' he said, 'it's hot here.' He took off his cap.

'Hey!' someone cried, 'hey, just take a look at that!'

There were shouts and calls and laughter and everyone pointed at the pilot. For on top of his head sat a bird. A starling. A sleeping starling.

'Ha ha! You look like a conjurer!' someone called.

Klee was woken by the noise and in an instant he was flying, high in the air, the blue air of summer in the south.

Of course, Klee never realized how he had got there, but his friends were even more surprised.

For when they came flying in, tired out, three days later, they saw Klee perched happily in the highest tree.

The Most Beautiful House in the World

Once upon a time an old man and an old woman lived together in a little house. They had a table and two chairs and a bed and a basket for the cat.

'After all, we don't need anything else,' said the woman. 'It would just be a burden to us.' And she went merrily off to sit in the sun with the cat on her lap.

But one day all their money had gone and they had to sell the two chairs.

'We don't need them at all, either,' said the woman. 'We can easily sit on the bed, it's much softer.' And she pushed the table alongside the bed. 'This is really cosy, after all,' she said, and she went to sit outside on the porch in the sun with the cat on her lap.

But one day all their money had gone again and they had to sell the table.

'What good is a table?' said the woman. 'We might just as well eat off the bedspread, since we're sitting on the bed. Look what a lot of space it gives us!' And she danced across the room with the cat in her arms.

But after a week there was nothing left of that money either.

'I can't find any work to earn some money,' said the man.

'It doesn't matter,' said the woman. 'We'll sell the bed. We might just as well sleep on the floor. It's healthy and good for your back, otherwise you grow crooked.'

And she walked to the fields with the cat to plait a coverlet of green grass. She stuck daisies in it and it looked wonderful.

But the man was so old that he couldn't even look for work any more and when the money for the bed had gone there was only the cat basket left to sell.

'That's really quite a good idea,' said the woman. 'It means that the cat can sleep between us. That makes it warm and cosy.'

But for the cat's basket they got no more than a florin, and that was gone in a day.

'Wife,' said the man, 'shall we sell the cat?'

'No,' said the woman. 'We will not sell the cat. It

would be much better to sell our house. It's much too big for us now, after all, with no table or chairs or bed or cat basket. We'll get on beautifully in a little hut.'

They sold their house and lived in a little hut for a whole year on the money.

'Ah, how lovely,' said the woman. 'So small. Everything close at hand. And I have much less to clean.' She went to sit in front of the hut in the sun, with the cat on her lap.

But when the year was over they had to sell the little hut and there was nothing left for them to live in.

'All right then,' said the woman. 'I'll make a little paper house. It's very easy and it doesn't cost much.'

She began to snip and stick, for three days. She cut out a front door with an arch and windows with frames and little lace curtains. She cut out a kitchen with pans and a stove, she cut out a sitting-room with a table and two chairs and a bed. She cut out a basket for the cat.

'Oh, how snug and cosy it is!' she cried, and then she stuck the whole little house together with a pretty gable at the front, and she cut a whole lot of fringes, snip-snip-snip along the eaves. They went in cautiously, so as not to tear it.

'But what if it rains now?' asked the man.

'Then we'll cut out a new one,' cried the woman, 'and we'll make it quite different. That will be lovely!' And she

24

clapped her hands with pleasure and stroked the cat in its paper basket.

But it did not rain. It blew. Hooi-hooi blew the wind, harder and harder, so hard that the little paper house was blown away and floated high up in the air.

'Look, husband!' cried the woman, 'now we are even flying. How lovely! See how beautiful the world down there is.' And she held up the cat to look through the paper window with them.

'We're going to fall,' cried the man fearfully.

'Yes!' his wife rejoiced, 'and who knows where we shall land!'

They landed a long, long way away, in a country where the sun was always shining. The wind set the little paper house down there, in the garden of a palace.

And the king who lived there found the little paper house so beautiful that he allowed it to stay there and everyone came to look. It was the most beautiful little house in the world.

The old man and the old woman were allowed to live in the palace, and so was the cat, in a real basket.

But he never lay in it. At night he slept between the woman and the man, nice and warm and cosy, and by day he sat on the woman's lap in the sun, on the porch of the king's palace.

The Squirrel People

On Sundays they always went picnicking, to a par-
ticular place in the wood where three tall beech trees stood.
Father, Mother, Olga and her little brothers. They played,
they romped, they looked for flowers and beech nuts and
acorns and chestnuts and they ate their sandwiches, each
from his own tin.

One day, when they were already sitting in the car ready
to drive home, Mother suddenly cried: 'Olga, your tin!
You have left your tin behind. Go and get it, quickly!'

Olga ran back along the woodland path, the way she
knew so well. In here, round that big oak tree, past the tall
bushes and, sure enough, there was her little tin. It sparkled

in the sunlight among the blades of grass. She picked it up and rushed back to the car.

She did not think of it again until she was in bed that night. Oh, help, the tin! She ought to have cleaned it out. If Mummy noticed tomorrow morning that the grease-proof paper and crumbs were still in it, Olga would be in trouble.

She crept quietly out of bed and down to the kitchen, snatched the tin off the table and raced upstairs again to her room on tiptoe. She opened the lid by the lamp above her bed and was about to turn the tin upside down over the wastepaper basket when she saw something extraordinary.

Two little feet, in black shoes and red stockings.

Olga quivered with astonishment and then sharply whipped away the piece of paper.

And there, on the bottom of the tin, was a tiny little fellow, lying in the breadcrumbs. He had fair hair and a brown face, wore a yellow jacket and green breeches, and he was holding a long blade of grass in his hand. His colours were all those of leaves in autumn.

'Hey!' squeaked the little fellow. 'Shut the door. There's a draught!'

'Th-the d-door?' stammered Olga.

'Yes! I mean . . .' Suddenly the little fellow sat upright. 'Oh no, I've overslept. Ooh, now I'll be in trouble!'

'Trouble?' asked Olga. 'Who from?'

But the little fellow did not answer. He was looking round the room, wide-eyed. 'Where is the wood?'

'The wood?' asked Olga. 'Did you come from the wood?'

'Yes, of course.'

'Are you a dwarf, then?'

'Of course not! Dwarves live under ground.'

'Where do you live, then?' asked Olga.

'In the trees, of course,' said the little fellow.

'Then who are you?' asked Olga.

'Who am I? I am Skitterbrook.'

Olga blinked. 'What?'

'Skit-ter-brook!' shouted the little fellow, suddenly furious. 'Skitterbrook who is always in trouble, Skitterbrook who has to do *this* and Skitterbrook who has to do *that*. Skitterbrook who has to look after the squirrels, feed the squirrels, wash the squirrels, clean the squirrels. Skitterbrook who gets blamed whenever a squirrel runs away and Skitterbrook who has to go and look for it. Now do you know?'

Olga's mouth had fallen wide open. 'Squirrels?' she asked.

'Yes, of course. You have horses, don't you?'

'We don't,' said Olga. 'We haven't got a horse.'

'No, but *people* have horses to ride on, don't they?' cried Skitterbrook peevishly. 'And you're a person, aren't you?'

'Yes,' said Olga in a low voice. 'I'm a little girl. I'm six.'

'Well, I'm twelve,' said Skitterbrook. 'And we have squirrels. But I'm not allowed on them. I just have to look after them. And keep an eye on them. But I'm going to be fine here.'

'Do you mean you got into my tin on purpose?' asked Olga. 'To run away?'

'Of course,' said Skitterbrook. 'And I'm staying here, too.'

'Oh,' said Olga.

'There,' said Skitterbrook, 'I want to live there.' He pointed to Olga's doll's house.

'Oh,' said Olga. 'Well, as long as you don't make any mess in there.'

Skitterbrook promised and Olga put the tin right by the front door so that Skitterbrook could walk straight in.

'Glory be!' he said. 'What a lovely room.' He ran straight upstairs and down again and up again. 'Can I sleep here?'

'No,' said Olga. 'That is Susan's bed. You must have the guest room.' She pointed it out and Skitterbrook immediately jumped onto the bed.

'It fits me perfectly,' he cried. 'But I haven't any pyjamas.'

Olga had a spare pair of doll's pyjamas for him and not long afterwards they were both tucked under the covers.

How extraordinary, thought Olga. How mad, how exciting, what fun! A real live squirrel man in my doll's house. If only no one sees him. If only my little brothers don't find him. If...

When Olga woke up next morning she did not remember at once what had happened the night before. But, as soon as she saw the sandwich tin standing on the chest of drawers beside the doll's house, she thought: Oh yes, Skitterbrook!

First she quickly cleaned out the little tin and put it on the table, then she peered into the doll's house guest room. Yes, look, there was the squirrel man, in bed. He was still snoring, should she let him sleep? No, better not. He would have to hide before anyone came into her room. She poked Skitterbrook in the side with a cautious finger.

He started up. 'Oh dear, has another one run away?' he squeaked.

'Sssh!' said Olga. 'Keep quiet and hide, otherwise they will see you.'

Skitterbrook also had to think for a moment before he remembered everything. 'Ooh!' he cried. 'Hip hip hooray! I'm here! I shan't have to clean any squirrels at all.'

'Yes,' whispered Olga, 'but you will have to hide. If my little brothers find you ...'

'Oh no,' said Skitterbrook. 'I'll stay in this fine house of yours. If anyone comes in I'll pretend to be a doll.'

Olga looked at him in surprise.

'Just like that one,' said Skitterbrook. He pointed to Susan and the other dolls sitting in chairs in Olga's doll's house. 'Then they'll think I'm one too.'

Olga thought this was dangerous, but Skitterbrook stretched out comfortably in his pyjamas and said: 'I want my breakfast in bed.'

Olga dressed quickly and before it was time to go to school she was just able to slip up to her room with half a sandwich.

'Here you are,' she whispered. 'It's got cheese spread on it.'

'Oh well,' said Skitterbrook, 'but it looks like a mattress. Couldn't you cut it into little bits?'

Olga had no time to listen to him. Her mother was calling impatiently, waiting to take her to school. At school Olga spent the whole time thinking about the squirrel man in her doll's house. 'Do stop dreaming, Olga,' her teacher kept telling her.

But all went well and that evening Skitterbrook told her about the wood he lived in. 'We have a big town, all built of branches, in a tall oak tree. Branch houses and branch streets and branch towers. And stables, of course, for the squirrels.'

'I've never seen a squirrel with anyone on its back,' said Olga.

'Well then, you've only seen the squirrels which have run away,' said Skitterbrook.

'Oh,' said Olga. 'And you're not allowed to ride them?'

'No,' said Skitterbrook. 'Only when I've got boots. Then I can.'

'Oh,' said Olga again. She fell asleep and next morning she brought him half a sandwich again, cut in chunks and with blackcurrant jam on it. 'How lovely!' said Skitter-brook.

That day went well too. No one discovered the squirrel man in the doll's house, but Olga saw that he had moved all the little chairs and tables and chests into different positions.

'You'll have to stop that,' she said. 'That's what you promised.'

'I'm so bored,' said Skitterbrook.

On Wednesday afternoon when Olga went up to her room, her little brothers were standing by the table. 'Where did you get the new doll?' they asked.

Olga was frozen with shock. 'Leave it alone!' she shouted.

Skitterbrook was lying on the table, motionless.

'What have you done with it?' she shouted.

'Nothing at all,' said her brothers. 'We've just looked. You can move all the different bits.'

'Where are his shoes?' cried Olga.

'He didn't have any shoes on,' said her brothers.

'Did!'

'Didn't!'

Olga's mother came in to put an end to the row. The boys were pushed out of the room. 'What is that nice little doll, Olga?' she asked.

'That's Skitterbrook,' said Olga. She began to cry.

'They've killed him. And they've taken his shoes away too.'

'Nonsense,' growled Skitterbrook. 'I'm not dead at all.'

But he continued to lie motionless and Olga's mother heard nothing because Olga was sobbing so loudly.

'Quiet, now,' she comforted, 'he's all in one piece. And I'll buy him some new shoes.'

'Boots!' squeaked Skitterbrook.

Mother did hear that, but she thought Olga had said it.

'Boots! That's a good idea, Olga!' she cried. 'They'll suit him beautifully. But you mustn't cry any more.'

Olga nodded, and when her mother had gone she picked Skitterbrook up.

'Did they hurt you at all?' she asked him.

'Don't fuss,' said Skitterbrook. 'Just bring me a bit of chocolate. For the shock.'

Olga did, and Skitterbrook went on living in the doll's house as though nothing had happened.

Next day Mother came home with some doll's boots. 'I hope they fit,' she said.

Olga rushed up to her room with them. Skitterbrook pulled them on and ran up and down the stairs three times in them. 'Like a glove!' he cried, which meant that they fitted perfectly. 'Hip hip hooray, now I can ride squirrels. Now I want to go back to the wood again.'

'Oh,' said Olga. 'Well, we'll be going for a picnic again

on Sunday. I'll take you with me.' And she thought: Perhaps then I shall see the town made of branches.

At last it was Sunday. At last they were going on a picnic. At last Olga could skip up quickly to her room and put Skitterbrook in her tin, among the sandwiches. 'Don't eat too much of them, will you?' she said.

They drove to the wood and spread out the rug under the three big beech trees. 'Let's play hide and seek!' cried Olga.

Everyone agreed. Father was going to do the seeking. 'I'll count to a hundred,' he said and he put his hands tightly over his eyes.

'Come on, Olga,' called her brothers, 'we know a good place.'

But Olga shook her head. 'I want to go alone,' she said.

While Father was still counting she quickly opened her tin, took out Skitterbrook and ran into the wood.

'Where is the town made of branches?' she asked him.

'Oh,' said Skitterbrook, 'it's a good bit farther on. Just put me down here.'

Olga did so.

'Good-bye, then,' said the squirrel man.

'Are you going right away now?' she asked. 'Shan't I ever see you again?' Suddenly she felt very sad. Having the

36

squirrel man in the doll's house in her room for a week had
been as much fun as having a real friend.

'Of course I'm going away,' said Skitterbrook. He bent
down, spat on his boots and polished them with his sleeve
until they shone. 'I'm going to ride squirrels. Good-bye.
Thanks a lot. I'm certainly going to be in trouble. I'd
better hurry now, been away a whole week.'

'Can't I . . .' Olga began, but Skitterbrook made off at
once. 'Can't I come with you? Oh, do wait!' she cried.
And without stopping to think she began to run after him.

In the distance she could hear her father calling: 'A
hundred! I'm coming!' But Olga had forgotten about hide
and seek. She raced after the little fellow, deeper and
deeper into the wood.

Skitterbrook was racing too. How the little fellow could
run, almost as fast as a squirrel, and you can't catch them
up. Olga ran as fast as she could. She got out of breath,
turned red in the face, began to feel tired and suddenly she
couldn't see him any more.

'Skitterbrook!' she shouted.

But all she could hear was a call in the distance: 'Olga!
Where are you? Come out!'

She ran on, looking to left and right. 'Now I've lost
him,' she thought. 'I shall never see him again.'

Then she looked up. She was standing under a tall, tall
oak tree and what did she see there? Squirrels, squirrels and

yet more squirrels, side by side along the branches, and then, oh look, the branches were branch streets and branch squares and branch houses and branch towers.

'The town!' thought Olga. 'That's the squirrel people's town of branches.'

'Skitterbrook!' she called up at the tree.

She tried to climb, but the trunk was too smooth. Suddenly she remembered something: 'Hey there!' she shouted up. 'Hey there, squirrel people! Skitterbrook isn't to get into trouble, do you hear? He's been away a long time, I know, but I couldn't bring him back any sooner and he's been very good and he's got boots and please will you let him ride the squirrels now too?'

There was still no sound from above.

'Hey there! Can you hear me?' asked Olga.

And suddenly she thought she must be dreaming.

The squirrels, which had run away when Olga began to shout, suddenly reappeared and began to climb down the trunk in a long procession. Each one with a little man on its back.

Olga took two steps backwards. They came galloping straight towards her and formed a big circle round her.

'Hello, human child!' said the little squeaky voices. 'You've brought back our good-for-nothing. Our thanks to you.' And all the little men took off their caps and bowed deeply. It was just like a circus.

'Oh hello, squirrel people!' cried Olga. 'What fun –'
But she didn't get any farther.

Suddenly voices were echoing through the wood. 'Olga, Olga, where are you?'

At tremendous speed the squirrels made off, the little men going bumpity bump on their backs. Only one had stayed where he was: Skitterbrook.

'Look here!' he cried proudly. '*My* squirrel! And I didn't get into trouble, luckily.' He gave the animal a nudge in the ribs with the heels of his boots. Before Olga knew what was happening the squirrel ran up her skirt and onto her shoulder and she felt a kiss from Skitterbrook planted on her cheek.

'Good-bye!' he squeaked.

Next moment he had vanished at a gallop between the tree trunks.

Olga was still staring straight ahead of her when her father and mother found her. 'Why did you hide so ridiculously far away?' they asked.

Later Olga tried to tell them all about it, but they did not believe her. 'You and your Skitterbrook!' teased her brothers. 'It was just an ordinary doll.'

Then Olga said no more. She often looked for the tree with the town of branches again, but she never found it. And whenever she saw a squirrel it was always a runaway squirrel, because there was never a little man on its back.

The Wonderful Dream-Teapot

Mrs Mole had a very fine house. It was under the ground, of course, because that is where moles live. Three rooms, a spacious hall, a little kitchen and up above a big mole hill; that was the front door.

It was very beautiful, and very lonely.

So the mole asked the mouse if she would not like to come and live with her there.

'You'll have a room of your own,' said the mole, 'and you will have to cook for me.'

'All right,' said the mouse.

But it was pitch dark in the mole's house, because moles don't need any light.

'I can't cook like this,' said the mouse, 'and I keep on bumping into things. Into the walls and into you. Just think, if I was holding a hot frying pan . . .'

So the mouse got a light in the kitchen and a light in her room and they lived together very snugly.

One day there was a knock at the front door, but, when the mouse opened it, instead of a visitor a hard nut came rolling in. And another, and another. Five nuts, ten nuts, helter-skelter into the spacious hall. And, smack bang, a couple of pine cones after them.

'Ow! What's this, what's going on?' cried the mole in a fright.

'I don't know, madam. Nuts and pine cones!' squeaked the mouse. 'They seem to be coming in by themselves.'

But they were not.

Outside there were seven squirrels and they were throwing the nuts in.

'That mole', said the squirrels, 'is living all alone in that big house. There's enough space there for our winter stores.'

And they threw another stack of nuts down through the mole hill, with ten acorns for good measure.

'Stop it, stop it!' moaned the mole.

The mouse retreated to the kitchen and the seven squirrels came in. They were very rude squirrels. 'We're going to take over the house!' they shouted. 'Clear off, mole! Dig yourself a new one!'

42

'Vandals!' cried Mrs Mole piteously, but it was no use. The squirrels brought light into the spacious hall and began to stack up the nuts and crab apples and acorns with a great deal of noise.

'We're going to settle down here!' they chanted, 'all winter long, all winter long!'

'Mouse!' cried the mole from her room, 'chase them away!'

'I don't dare to!' wailed the mouse from the kitchen.

'Ha ha!' cried the squirrels, 'there's a mouse in here too!'

And they flung open the kitchen door so that the mouse had to come out and the bedroom door so that the mole had to come out and the seven of them chased the poor mole and the poor mouse out of the front door.

'Ow!' cried the mole. 'Ow, the light hurts my eyes. I can't see anything!'

The mouse took her by the hand and they fled into the wood.

'Oh, oh,' wept the mole, 'don't leave me alone.'

'No, madam,' said the mouse. 'I'm going to look for a good place where you can dig a new house.'

'Oh, oh,' wept the mole, 'I'm far too tired.'

'Then I shall look for a little hole', said the mouse, 'to sleep in.'

At that moment there was a rustling in the dry leaves and a strange voice said: 'Hoy hoy, little mistress, you'd better stay away from me.'

'Who, who, what, who's there?' cried the mole nervously. She was stone-blind in the light.

'It's a hedgehog, madam,' said the mouse. And it was. A circular hedgehog in a circular coat of prickles.

'Oh, Mr Hedgehog!' cried Mrs Mole, putting out her hand. 'Where are you? Ow!'

Her fingers touched the prickly coat and it was sharp.

'Hoy hoy, little lady, you really must keep away from me.'

'Yes,' said the mouse, 'but madam is short-sighted,' and she told the hedgehog everything that had happened to them.

'Squirrels, bah!' said the hedgehog. 'Come along with

me and we'll find a fine warm sleeping hole for the night.'

And off they went, Mrs Mole between the mouse and the hedgehog. They led her carefully by the hand, further and further into the wood.

But a hole was not so easy to find.

There were plenty of little ones, but the three of them could not get in.

'I'm getting very tired,' complained the mole.

'Just lean on me, madam,' said the mouse.

Poor mouse, she almost collapsed, but Mrs Mole did not dare to lean on the hedgehog.

Then they found a hole, a big hole, a beautiful hole, a spacious hole. It was under a big beech tree and they could get in easily.

'Is it empty?' asked Mrs Mole.

'Yes, yes, come on in,' said the hedgehog.

The mole put her arms out and felt along the walls. 'Oh!' she cried, 'Oh, oh, what's that?'

She was tapping against something made of wood.

Before the mouse and the hedgehog could answer, they heard the chink of locks and the squeak of hinges. The mole had been tapping on a door and now the door was slowly opening.

'What's all this about?' asked a harsh voice.

Before them stood a gnome with a long white beard and a lantern in his hand.

'What's all this about?' asked the gnome again.

The mole, the mouse and the hedgehog had not said anything at all, they were so astonished to find a door in the hole under the beech tree.

'Oh,' squeaked the mouse, 'we only wanted to sleep here.'

'I see,' said the gnome. 'Then why did you knock at the door?'

'I–I did that by mistake,' said the mole.

But the hedgehog cried: 'Door? What do you mean?'

The gnome put down his lantern and stroked his white beard. 'Didn't you know', he said, 'that this was the door to the underground city of the gnomes?'

'What?' replied the mole. 'What did you say, city? A city with houses? Is there a house for me? I'm looking for a house.'

46

'Psha!' said the gnome.

'Well, you see,' began the mouse, 'Mrs Mole has been thrown out, by some rough squirrels. Thrown out of her own house, by seven squirrels throwing nuts and acorns and all kinds of hard things. And now . . .'

'The city is full,' said the gnome.

'Hoy hoy,' cried the hedgehog. 'There must surely be one house left? Couldn't we go and have a look?'

The gnome stroked his beard again.

'You will have to ask the king first,' he said.

'The king?' cried Mrs Mole. 'Is the king a nice king?'

'Come with me,' said the gnome.

They followed the bent little man through the door, down a long passage, three steps down and then . . . then they saw the underground city of the gnomes. Houses, streets, squares, towers and a palace. And above it, instead of the blue sky, arched the yellow sand of the wood, with trailing roots poking through it everywhere.

'Oh!' cried the mole, 'so light, so light! I can't see anything.'

The mouse and the hedgehog had to guide her again, one on each side, because there were hundreds of glow worms crawling down the streets and on the houses, and hundreds of fireflies flying through the air, and all the little lights were going on-off, on-off, so that it almost made you dizzy.

The three animals walked into the underground city behind the doorkeeper, and all the gnomes peared through the windows of their little houses and muttered: 'A mole, a mouse and a hedgehog? What are they doing here, what are they doing here?'

In the palace there were still more lights and the mole kept crying: 'Well, where is the king?' And she made a deep bow before every pillar because she thought it was the king. But when at last they were standing before the king she asked: 'Ah, is that the kitchen stove?' so that the mouse had to say quickly: 'No, madam, the king.'

'Oh, oh,' cried the mole, 'Don't be angry with me, Sire, my eyes are so poor in the light. I'm a mole you see, I live in darkness, but I haven't got a house any more and I wanted to ask you . . .'

'Ho, ho, ho,' said the king. He had a deep voice and he was wearing a flame-red cloak and a crown of twigs and green leaves on his head and he was sitting on a seat of moss covered with little white flowers.

'Doorman,' said the king, 'who are these?'

The gnome with the lantern told him the whole story.

'So, so, so, so, so, so, so,' said the king seven times in a row. 'A house? There just happens to be one at the edge of the town. Empty. You can move in. But –' he held up one finger – 'if you don't behave nicely, I shall put you in prison. All three of you. And you can cry your eyes out there for the rest of your lives. Doorman, take them there.'

'T-to prison?' asked the mouse with a squeak of terror.

But it was not to prison. The doorman took them to an empty house at the edge of the town. An old house, a lopsided house, a junk house, with three rooms and a kitchen.

They made one room dark for Mrs Mole, one light for the hedgehog, and the mouse had to live in the kitchen because it was her job to do the cooking.

'Then we'll keep the third room for best,' said the hedgehog. 'For when we have visitors.'

Mrs Mole went to bed at once. The hedgehog rolled himself up and the mouse began to polish and clean and scrub and sweep and scour and scratch until the whole house shone like a mirror.

Next morning the mouse went to market to buy food and to all the gnomes she said, very politely: 'Good morning, gnome sir,' and then they all answered: 'Good morning mouse, just call me gnome,' in a very friendly way.

The mouse also brought paint to decorate the house. The hedgehog helped, but the mole did not, because she would have painted red over yellow and green over blue and made everything hideous.

They lived in great comfort. For a whole week, and then another week.

49

Then a letter arrived.

'What does it say, what does it say?' asked Mrs Mole. She had opened it and was holding the paper upside down. 'I can't read it.'

The hedgehog read out:

'Dear Mrs Mole,
      I shall pay you a visit tomorrow afternoon. I am coming to tea.

The King.'

'What?' cried the mouse. 'The king? The king's coming to see us? Help, then I shall have to clean and polish and dust and sweep and wash the cups. For, oh, if everything is not neat and tidy we shall have to go to prison and cry our eyes out all our lives . . .'

There was quite a procession when the king of the gnomes came to drink tea with them. Twelve trumpeters walked in front, and behind them marched seven lid-clashers, a big drum and a kettledrum. The whole street shuddered with tarantara and zingboom.

Three lackeys pressed the bell at once. The mouse did not dare to open the door, but the hedgehog did. 'Good afternoon, Your Majesty,' he said, 'hoy hoy, how agreeable to see you here.'

'So, so so, so, so, so, so,' said the king seven times in a

row, and he wiped his feet on the mat. 'It looks charming in here, charming.'

He walked all round the house. The kitchen shone, the hedgehog's room gleamed, Mrs Mole's room was pitch-black.

'Hum?' asked the king.

'Yes, you see,' explained the mouse, 'Mrs Mole lives in the dark. That's why.'

'Oh yes, just so,' said the king.

Then they went into the third room, the best room, the room for visitors. There sat Mrs Mole in her well-cleaned party dress. 'Oh, oh, I can see nothing, I can see nothing!' she cried, 'but you are sure to be the king.'

She made a deep bow.

'Please sit down, Sir King,' and she pointed to the mouse as if she were a chair.

The poor mouse did not dare to move, for she thought it might be very genteel to have the king sitting on her. But the king said: 'Hello, mouse,' and took the armchair which had been put ready for him.

'A cup of tea, Sir King?' asked Mrs Mole.

'Yes, yes,' squeaked the mouse. 'I will pour out.' And she was already on her feet.

But the king held her back. 'Is tea already made?' he asked.

'Yes, in the big pot,' said the mouse.

The king laughed mysteriously.

'I have a better pot,' he said. 'A present. For you.'

And from under his red cloak the king took a gleaming, sparkling, brand-new, real silver teapot. 'Here you are!'

'What is that? What is that?' cried the mole.

'Oh madam, a real beauty!' cried the mouse.

'Hoy hoy, thank you very much, Sir King,' said the hedgehog.

The mouse put fresh tea in the fresh pot and poured out a cup for everyone. The most beautiful cup, with the gold rim, was for the king. They drank. And then it happened.

'Oh, oh!' cried Mrs Mole, 'how lovely! I can see everything, what dazzling magnificence in this room!' She began to dance round and round.

And the king began to laugh: 'Ha ha, now I can play the

fool!' and he hopped across the room on one leg and pulled peculiar faces.

The mouse was sitting on the table, singing with all her might: 'I'm not afraid, not afraid of anyone, never more afraid, afraid!'

The hedgehog lay down on his back with flattened prickles and with his bare tummy upwards. 'Come and tickle me,' he cried, 'come and tickle me, I shall love it!'

The party became odder, the more tea they drank. They no longer called the king 'Your Majesty', they pushed each other giggling into the chairs, they played hide and seek all over the house and 'Coo-ee, can't catch me', and they danced on the beds.

Out in the street the gnomes from the royal retinue stood stiffly to attention, with their trumpets and their clashing-lids and kettledrums, ready to start making music as soon as the king came out.

'The king has important things to do in there,' they thought.

But the king was calling 'Cuckoo' from behind the chest of drawers and jumping onto the sofa, making Mrs Mole fly into the air with a shriek.

Not until the teapot was completely empty did they come to their senses.

'Thank you very much for your visit,' said Mrs Mole. 'It was most agreeable.'

'Likewise,' said the king politely.

'I will show you to the door,' said the hedgehog.

'I'm so sorry about the mess,' whispered the mouse, 'I-I-I . . .'

But the king spoke: 'This teapot is a wonderful dream teapot. I got it from a wizard. Guard it well. From now on I shall come and take tea with you every week in this house. Because you will understand that I can never do it in the royal palace . . .'

And with a great royal wink he vanished up the street, behind the marching music.

The mouse tidied up the whole house and put the wonderful dream teapot high up, on the topmost shelf in the kitchen, in a safe place.

'Remember,' said Mrs Mole, 'we must never speak of this. To anyone.'

'Hoy hoy, no!' cried the hedgehog.

And they did not speak of it. To anyone.

Yet something happened which made the next tea party with the king of the gnomes quite different . . .

Something terrible happened. On Sunday afternoon Mrs Mole said: 'Mouse, I have thought of something delightful. Make a cup of tea in the wonderful dream teapot.'

'Oh yes,' cried the hedgehog.

The mouse went to the kitchen but, instead of putting the water on, she gave a shriek. 'The teapot! The teapot has gone!'

'What?' the hedgehog stormed into the kitchen.

Mrs Mole shouted angry things. All three of them searched, the mole knocking everything over and the mouse saying every time: 'Oh madam, how terrible.'

'Yes, terrible,' said Mrs Mole. 'How can it have gone?'

But the king's silver teapot was nowhere to be found. They searched all through the house. And time and again Mrs Mole cried: 'I've got it, I've got it!' but she always had a flower pot in her hand or a vase, or a watering can. She was so dreadfully blind.

'How awful!' sobbed the mouse. 'It must have been stolen.'

'Stolen? How can that be? By whom?'

They couldn't think. The door was always firmly locked at night and the windows tightly shut.

'Ooh!' cried the mouse suddenly, 'what are we to do when the king comes next week?'

They had not thought of that yet. The king was to come every week, to drink tea from the wonderful dream teapot and be able to hop about merrily on one leg and call 'Cuckoo' from behind the chest of drawers.

'We'll have to buy a new one,' said the hedgehog.

The mouse went to market the following day but,

wherever she asked for a wonderful dream teapot, they laughed at her, or shook their heads. None of the gnomes had ever heard of such a teapot. 'It must be some magic thing,' they said, 'we haven't got anything like that here.'

Then the mouse bought an ordinary teapot, a green one, rather like the real one. And she bought expensive silver paint.

'Hoy hoy,' said the hedgehog, 'bright idea!' And together they painted the green teapot silver. It looked almost genuine.

'What on earth are you doing?' cried the mole.

'We have copied the teapot, madam. There's practically no difference.'

'Oh,' cried the mole, 'but will it give us wonderful dreams as well? Because of the tea? Surely not. And when the king notices that, we shall have to go to prison,' she moaned, 'and cry our eyes out all our lives.'

'Hoy hoy,' said the hedgehog, 'then we must behave as if we were feeling merry.'

On Tuesday afternoon the king came. One-two, the gnomes marched ahead of him and tarantara zingboom went their trumpets and lids and kettledrums. 'Oh, oh, here he is already!' cried Mrs Mole, and she began to dance right away, but it was too soon.

'Is tea made?' asked the king as soon as he was inside.

'Eh, eh yes,' said the mouse, trembling, and she poured

out four cups of tea from the silver-painted green imitation pot.

'Aha,' said the king, 'then the festivities can begin again.'

He took a mouthful, with royal dignity. Mrs Mole took a mouthful, with her little finger held stiffly in the air. The mouse took a little mouthful, which went down her throat with a loud gulp. The hedgehog took two mouthfuls and immediately shouted: 'Yodeli-ee-tee!'

'Pardon?' said the king. He drew down his eyebrows and looked very starchy.

'Whoops!' cried Mrs Mole, beginning to bounce on the sofa.

'What did you say, lady?' said the king. He sat very straight and looked very stern.

'Eekety-eek!' squeaked the mouse and jumped onto the lamp with a screech.

'Ah hum,' said the king. He finished his cup stiffly and stood up.

'Hoy!' cried the hedgehog, 'me old buffer!' and he tweaked the king's beard.

The king turned white with rage. 'What is the meaning of this?' he thundered.

'The tea!' whimpered Mrs Mole, 'the wonderful dream tea. Don't you feel merry?'

No, the king did not feel merry. 'Not in the least,' he cried. 'Absolutely not,' he shouted. 'Cheats!' he cried, 'where is the teapot? What have you done with it?'

There was no help for it. The king snatched the tea cosy off so violently that the pot overturned and the hot tea gushed out over his left foot.

'Ouch! ouch!' There was the king, dancing round the room on one leg. Yes, he was. But not because he had wonderful dreams. It was no dream. The teapot was covered with scratches, he could see that quite well, scratches in the silver, but it was not silver, it was paint.

'Cheats!' bellowed the king again.

'Oh, please,' whimpered Mrs Mole, 'we can't help it!'

'The real one has been stolen,' explained the hedgehog.

'From my kitchen,' squeaked the mouse.

'Stolen?' bellowed the king. 'By whom?'

'We don't know,' moaned the mole.

'Everything was locked,' explained the hedgehog.

'And the windows tight shut,' squeaked the mouse.

The king sank with a plop onto the sofa, which sent Mrs Mole flying into the air. Oh yes. But not for joy. There was no joyfulness, because the king said: 'If you do not find the thief, if you do not get the silver teapot back by next week, you will go to prison. All three of you.'

Mrs Mole began to weep at once.

But the king went away with angry strides and slammed the door behind him with an angry crash.

Tarantara went the trumpeters and zingboom went the kettledrums and one-two marched the gnomes down the street with the king.

The mole, the mouse and the hedgehog were left behind in deathly silence. How were they to find the thief in a week's time . . .?

They had exactly seven days, the mole, the mouse and the hedgehog, to find the thief who had stolen the wonderful dream teapot. On the first day they searched the whole house once more, to make sure that the pot was not really hidden away in some remote corner.

But no.

The second day the mouse went to market to ask once again if anyone had seen a silver teapot.

But no.

The third day the mole asked the gnomes in the street if there were any thieves living in the underground city. 'No,' they said, 'there are no thieves living here.'

The fourth day the hedgehog went to the doorman under the beech tree to ask if any other strangers had come to the city. 'No,' said the doorman, 'no gnomes and no animals.'

The fifth day the three of them examined the front door of their house all over again, and all the windows, to see if there were any marks or traces of the thief to be seen. But no, nothing to be seen.

The sixth day they told each other: 'We shall never find the thief, because there can't have been a thief at all.'

The seventh day all three of them sat crying. The mole in her dark room, the hedgehog in the pretty room and the mouse in the kitchen.

That afternoon the king would be coming, they thought, and they would have to go to prison to spend the rest of their lives crying their eyes out there.

'Oh, oh,' sobbed the mouse, 'there he is already!' Because she could hear banging and thought it was the procession of marching gnomes, with the king.

But the banging was not coming from the street.

It was coming from above. A little white sand actually fell down from the kitchen ceiling.

'Ah,' thought the mouse.

60

She stood up and looked at the ceiling. And then – then she saw something strange. In the sandy ceiling, just above the uppermost shelf, on the very spot where the wonderful dream teapot had stood, there was a hole. Really a kind of mouse hole. She would be able to get through it easily.

'Aha,' thought the mouse and, without giving a further thought to where she might end up, she jumped onto the topmost shelf and crept into the little hole.

'Of course, this is the way the thief came,' she thought. 'Now I shall find him!'

The hole became a passage and finally a broad corridor, full of light, and suddenly the mouse stood stock still. She knew where she was. She ... She ... 'It can't be!' squeaked the mouse, for she had arrived in the lovely, big, spacious house of Mrs Mole. The one they had been thrown out of by seven squirrels. It lay exactly over their little house in the underground city and the banging and calls of 'Cuckoo' came from the squirrels. They had stolen the wonderful dream teapot and now they were drinking tea from it, dancing and hopping on one leg.

The mouse peeped round a corner and sure enough, there they were, the seven of them. On the tables, on the expensive sofa and hanging from the light. Seven brown squirrels, their feathery tails sticking up in the air with pleasure. Yodeli-ee-tee! and atishootoo, and the silver teapot was standing on a table in the middle.

The mouse was so furious when she saw this that she became the bravest mouse in the world. With a great leap she flew under the tea table, picked it up and began to run with it.

'Help!' yelled the squirrels. 'A ghost! It's a magic teapot!' They had not seen the mouse at all.

'Look out!' shrieked the squirrels and the teapot fell over, so that they got hot tea over their toes.

'Ow, ow!' yelled the squirrels and, hopping on the other leg, they ran from the house, all seven of them. The front door slammed to with a crash behind them.

But the mouse had no time to be pleased. She picked up the fallen teapot, rushed down the corridor with it into the small passage, through the hole and fell crash bang wallop

with all the pots and pans off the shelf onto the kitchen
floor.

'Who's there, what's that?' cried Mrs Mole.

'Hoy hoy!' cried the hedgehog.

'A thief!' cried Mrs Mole and she came blundering into
the room followed by the hedgehog.

'I've got him!' cried Mrs Mole, and grabbed the mouse
by the tail.

'No madam!' cried the mouse, 'it's me. Let me go. I
must put the water on! I . . .'

'Tarantara!' resounded from the street. The procession
of gnomes was approaching with the king.

Half an hour later the mouse was at last able to tell the
whole story in peace to the king, the mole and the hedgehog.

'So, so, so, so, so, so, so,' said the king seven times in a
row. 'So now you have two houses. One here in the city
and one up there in the wood. That's nice. Pour me out a
cup of tea do, brave mouse.'

They drank tea all afternoon and they had the most wonderful dreams. They leaped and danced and called each
other by their first names and called 'Cuckoo' from behind
the chest of drawers. Mrs Mole could see everything in the
bright light, the hedgehog bared his tummy to be tickled,
the mouse sang full-throatedly of her lack of fear and the
king swung on the lamp.

Since then the mole, the mouse and the hedgehog have lived in two houses at once. The wonderful dream teapot stands in a special case with a sturdy lock on it. Once a week the king of the gnomes comes to visit them and to clown around, because he can never do that in his palace.

And if you ever see a hedgehog dancing through the wood on one leg, you will know that he has just made himself a cup of tea. For he sometimes does that. Hoy hoy!

The Rocking Horse

The rocking horse was made of wood and the children rode all day on his wooden back. Rocketty-rock by the window, until the trees and the houses outside danced up and down. The children rode to Spain, to Africa and to the moon, but the rocking horse was sad, for his nose was made of wood and his eyes were painted. He could not see Spain, nor Africa, nor the moon, and he could not nuzzle the children.

One night a fairy passed by the window and turned the rocking horse, abracadabra! into a real horse.

There he stood, with a brown, quivering coat, in the nursery. Snores came from the two little beds and the horse could hear them.

Moonlight shone through the window and the horse could see it. And there was the fairy, her wings of dazzling gauze.

'Thank you so very much,' said the horse.

'It's only for night-time,' said the fairy. 'By day you'll be wooden again. The children must never know.'

'Will I be a horse every night?'

'Yes, yes,' said the fairy, 'and you can go out then too.

But not too far. You must be back in this room before it's light.'

'Thank you so very much,' said the horse.

On the first night he went to the park to graze.

On the second night to the meadow to gallop.

On the third night to the wood, but before he left he actually nuzzled the snoring children in their little beds.

By day he was made of wood and the children rode on his back, to Spain, to Africa and to the moon.

The next night, when the horse wrinkled his nose against the little boy's cheek again, the little boy woke up. 'Hallo, rocking horse!'

The little girl woke up too. 'Hallo, rocking horse! Are

you not rocking but real now? Can we ride you and really go out?'

'Yes,' cried the little boy, 'now, this minute,' and he climbed onto the horse's back in his pyjamas and the little girl climbed up behind him in her nightdress. The horse jumped out of the window and galloped to the park and he could feel the two warm children's bodies on his back. The little boy held tight to the horse's neck and the little girl to the little boy's waist, for they were travelling fast.

But in the park he slowed down, for the moon had flown with them through the air and was shining on the trees with great beauty. They made blue shadows in the grass. 'Now we're in Spain,' said the little boy.

But the fairy was standing in front of them. She was angry. 'The children were not allowed to know,' she said. 'I shall turn you back into a wooden horse for punishment.'

The horse hung his head and the children began to cry.

'It's so nice,' they sobbed. 'Please let it be a horse for now. We won't tell anyone.'

'Just this time then,' said the fairy. 'Home at once, and don't let me see you on his back at night again!'

The horse galloped back and the children crept into bed.

But next night the little boy and the little girl could not go to sleep, and when it struck midnight they heard the rocking horse whinny.

'Are you alive again?'

The horse nodded.

They jumped out of bed, stroked his nose and climbed on his back.

'It was so lovely yesterday,' the little boy whispered in the horse's ear. 'If you go the other way, the fairy won't see us.'

The horse went the other way and they came to the meadow, where he took great jumps. The children shrieked with laughter and the horse jumped over a ditch.

'The other side is Africa!' shouted the little boy, but on the other side stood the fairy. She was furious. 'You were not allowed to take the children out with you at night any more,' she cried. 'I shall turn you back into a wooden horse for punishment.'

'No, no!' cried the children. 'Please, fairy. We will never never do it again!'

'Then this is for the last time,' said the fairy. 'If I see you once again, he will never turn into a horse any more.'

On the third night the children did not even go to bed but stayed on the rocking horse's back. And when the clock struck twelve they felt the wooden back grow warm and turn to hair.

'Stay indoors, horse!' they cried, 'and run in circles on the carpet.'

But the moon shone so terribly bright and the summer sun smelled so sweet that after three rounds the horse

68

jumped over the window-sill and galloped straight for the wood.

'Are we on the moon now?' asked the little boy. But the horse shook his head and stopped to listen to the nightingales and to the wind rustling in the tree-tops. They stood still for an hour and they wandered about for an hour, across the white patches of light and through the dark shadows, and then they had to go home, for it would soon be light.

'Hold on tight,' said the horse, 'for I shall fly as fast as a bird.'

But before the window of their nursery stood the fairy. She lifted her arms and cried: 'Abracadabra, bang!' and when the horse jumped into the room he landed with a hard bang. 'Ow!' cried the children, for the horse's back was made of wood.

Since then the children no longer ride their rocking horse. He stands stock-still all day inside the room, looking sadly out of his painted eyes. Only at night the little boy still sometimes gets out of bed and rides rocketty-rock on his wooden back. Then the moon outside dances up and down and the little boy hopes that the horse will carry him to it.

But the horse remains a rocking horse and the fairy will never come back.

The Witch's Shoes

Once upon a time there was a little boy. His name was Alexander Jackson Popp, and he was a very funny little boy. When it had been raining, he stamped hard in all the puddles to make them splash. And when he saw a dignified-looking lady coming towards him he would pull monkey faces.

One day Alexander Jackson Popp went for a walk in the wood. Not too far, because that was not allowed, but far enough to pick blackberries, because he was fond of blackberries. He also liked the purple fingers you get when you pick blackberries. When he pricked himself on a thorn he shouted: 'Ow, bobberdejob!'

Then he saw a pair of shoes lying under a blackberry bush. Old shoes.

Alexander Jackson Popp bent down and stretched his arm out cautiously to pick up the shoes. 'Ow, bobberdejob, ow!' he shouted, pulling them out.

'Now, who would take off his shoes under a blackberry bush?' he thought, and he put them on. Over his own shoes, for they were quite big enough. 'Hey, whoops!' cried Alexander Jackson Popp, for he had suddenly begun to run. To skip and scamper and gallop, whether he wanted to or not. 'Whoa there!' he cried, 'stop!' But he couldn't stop.

The shoes carried him on, deeper into the wood.

Then Alexander Jackson Popp sat down on the ground with his legs in the air and tried to pull off the shoes. But it was no use. They simply went on skipping and his legs had to obey. He looked like a little boy bicycling on his back, 'I must be a funny sight,' he thought and began to laugh.

'Wait a bit!' He turned over and scrambled to his feet. 'I'll run home now,' he thought, but he didn't.

The shoes made him run back again in a big half-circle, farther into the wood.

'All right then, let's see where we land up. Perhaps I shall find a treasure,' he thought. But the shoes carried him straight to the witch's house. The door was open and biff bang wallop, without wiping his feet, the funny little boy thundered straight into the room. Oof, poof, at last they were standing still.

The witch was sitting by the fire.

'Oh,' she said, 'thank you for bringing back my shoes.'

'Are they yours, then?'

'Naturally. They're magic shoes, aren't they? Just take them off now.'

'Oh,' said Alexander Jackson Popp, 'are you a magic witch, then?'

'Naturally. Or the shoes wouldn't come back to me, would they?'

'Oh. Can you go anywhere in magic shoes?'

'Naturally. What else would they be good for?'

'Can you go anywhere in the world in them?'

'Yes, well, take them off now,' said the witch.

'Couldn't I have another go in them?'

'Take them off!'

Alexander Jackson Popp sat down on a chair and tugged at the right shoe. He tugged and tugged, his face turned red and he was panting, uh, uh. But he was only pretending. Then he tried the left one. 'Uh uh! Bobberdejob, they won't come off. You have a go.'

The witch squatted down in front of him but, just as she was about to give the shoes a tug, Alexander Jackson Popp

gave her a shove with his feet, so that she fell back on her witch's bottom.

'Squib squab!' she squawked; that is an awful witch's word, but Alexander Jackson Popp pulled a face at her, jumped to his feet and shouted very loudly to the magic shoes: 'I want to go through all the puddles in the world and have a lovely splash!'

Instantly he shot out of the room, through the door and into the wood. His legs were going as fast as a fly's wings. All he could see was a blur. In one moment he was in Holland, where it had just been raining, and he went splash splash through all the puddles there.

'Bobberdejob, this is great!' cried the little boy, and his trousers were soaking wet. Then he was running through Belgium and when his shirt was soaking wet as well he ran through the puddles of France.

'I'm never going to give these shoes back,' he thought to himself. 'What fun this is! If I keep them, I can play "He" in them too and I shall always win.'

He skipped over mountains and straight across rivers and even bits of sea. But not through the desert, for everything is as dry as a bone there. The deepest puddles were in Indonesia. Splash, splash, and then Alexander Jackson Popp wanted to go home.

'Home again!' he shouted to the magic shoes.

But the shoes did not turn round, for they had not yet

done all the puddles in the world. How many puddles can there be in the whole world? In Australia and Africa and America and Puddleby-on-the-Marsh and in front of the post office. The shoes did not miss any of them. Only at the last puddle, in Littlemoping, did they stop, at last.

'Bobberdejob,' said Alexander Jackson Popp. 'I'm so tired. And wet.' The water of the whole world was dripping from his clothes. 'I shall have to go home now.'

No sooner had he spoken when the shoes began to run again. But not to the house where Alexander Jackson Popp lived. To the witch's house, because that is where they belonged.

Biff bang, there he was, back in the witch's room. The witch was sitting by the fire.

'Oh,' she said. 'Have you brought them back at last? Are you wet through?'

'Yes.'

'Take them off then.'

Alexander Jackson Popp sat down. He pulled at the right shoe. He tugged and tugged, but now it really wouldn't come off. The shoes were too wet. They had to dry by the fire for an hour and then at last they came off. Alexander Jackson Popp got home late. His mother was cross with him.

'Where have you been all this time?' she asked.

Now you try telling the story!

74

The Giant

A very long way from here, at the foot of a high mountain, lies a village. On the mountain lived a giant, and every night the giant came to fetch water in the village. The people heard his footsteps booming down the street and they heard him rattling his pails by the well.

'He makes such a row,' said the people, 'and he takes so much water every time. This has got to stop.' But no one dared to go up the mountain to tell the giant he was not to come any more. No one had ever seen the giant, because he always came when it was pitch-dark.

'We shall have to catch him,' said someone.

'How?' asked another.

'With rope.'

But they had no rope strong enough for a giant, except for the bell rope, and the verger refused to give that up. 'I wouldn't be able to ring any more,' he said.

The carpenter had an idea. 'We'll do it with glue,' he said.

That evening he covered the street where the giant always walked with wood glue. That is the strongest glue there is. And, when the giant came that night, the people heard a terrible noise and a wicked giant's word. No one dared to go and look. But a little later they heard the rattling of the buckets again and next morning the well was half empty.

But on the patch of glue stood two shoes, stuck fast. A huge giant's left shoe and a huge big giant's right shoe.

'Let's try again,' said the carpenter, and he put down some more glue in another place.

The giant came in the middle of the night; the noise was worse than before, two awful giant's words resounded through the streets, but once again the people heard the buckets rattling by the well. Almost all the water had gone next morning and on the patch of glue stood two boots. A giant left boot and a giant right boot, stuck fast in the middle of the street. They looked like a gateway.

'Next time we'll have him,' said the carpenter, and this time he spread the glue close to the well.

The giant came, stepping softly and warily, but still the people heard him, because everyone was awake. So they also heard the three awful giant's words he muttered.

'We've got him,' thought the carpenter, but there went the buckets, clack-clatter-clack and, alack and alas, next morning the well was quite empty. On the patch of glue stood two socks, bolt upright, because they were made of sheep's wool. A giant's left woollen sock and a giant's right woollen sock.

'Poor man,' said the carpenter's wife. 'Now he's up there on the mountain in his bare feet.'

'Just what I wanted,' cried the carpenter. 'You wait!' And that evening he covered the whole square round the well with his strongest glue.

Plop plop, there was the giant again, at twelve midnight, and scarcely had he reached the well when he set up a pitiful roar.

'We've got him, we've got him!' all the people shouted and they rushed out of their houses in their pyjamas and nightdresses and without their slippers. 'Hurrah, hurrah, we've caught the giant!' They held hands to dance around the giant. They couldn't even see him in the darkness, they could only hear him.

No, they didn't see anything in the darkness, and they didn't think, either. Not even of the glue.

Squidge squelch squash, there they were, caught fast in the square themselves, in their bare feet, just like the giant.

Then awful giant words and awful human words were all jumbled together until it was morning and they could see each other.

'Ha ha!' bellowed the giant, and he began to shake with laughter. 'It's your own fault!'

The awestruck people looked at his legs, which had hair as thick as twigs. At his trousers, as big as a sailing ship, his jersey, which was like a ploughed field, and at his face. What a face that giant had! His nose was a bridge, and you could have gone for a walk on his cheeks.

'I can reach the water easily,' said the giant. 'But you can't.'

He leaned right over and scooped up a bucketful, drinking it off as if it were a mug.

'You are very nasty people,' said the giant. 'Why did you put down that glue?'

'So that you wouldn't make such a row at night,' screamed the people. 'And because you take so much water.'

'But the well fills itself up again, doesn't it?' said the giant.

'Yes, but we can't get to sleep at night,' shouted the people.

'You should have told me,' said the giant. 'I would have been quiet about it then.'

He drank a couple more bucketfuls, slurping and slopping the water about. It ran down his chin and dripped to the ground beside his feet, making the glue soft. So soft that the giant was able to pull his feet out. 'There,' he said, 'you just stay where you are. I'm going home, up the mountain. Good-bye.'

He worked his socks and boots and shoes loose as well and left the village.

The people of the village had to stand stock-still all day, stuck fast to the square round the well. No one could get to the water; no one could get away.

That evening the giant came back again with his empty buckets.

'Oh, please, Mr Giant,' cried the carpenter's wife, 'we will never do it again. Do please get us loose. You can always come to fetch water, as much as you want.'

'Come on, then,' said the giant. 'You have had your punishment.' And he splashed water over them until they could soak off the glue.

From then on the giant came to fetch water by day. The people of the village always greeted him politely, because he was really an awfully nice giant.

The Paper Palace

Caroline had a bad leg and it kept her in bed for a long time. She was fearfully bored, because she had read all her books and used up all her paints.

Then her grandmother bought her a present. A nice present: a pair of scissors.

'For my nails?' asked Caroline.

'No,' said Grandmother. 'To cut things out of paper.'

'What kind of things?' asked Caroline.

'People,' said Grandmother. 'And animals and trees and houses and anything you can think of.'

It was not at all easy. First Caroline cut out a car, but it looked more like a jam jar on legs. Then she made a hare and a rabbit, but they looked more like funny hats.

She took a new sheet of paper and cut out another animal.

'Did *you* make that dog?' her father asked. 'With your grandmother's scissors? Jolly good!'

Caroline practised and practised and after a week she could cut out anything she liked with the scissors. Even little houses, which she would cut out and then stick together. Everyone had heard about it and everyone in the neighbourhood came to look. There was the farm which sick little Caroline had made, with barns and stables and chickens and cows and pigs. And ducks, in a silver paper pond.

'Good gracious, Caroline, how clever!'

One night Caroline had a strange dream. A tiny little man, smaller than her little finger, skipped onto the table. 'You must make a palace,' he said.

'A palace?' asked Caroline. 'What for?'

'For the queen,' said the little man. 'In three days' time she is giving a party and it's got to be in a beautiful new palace.'

'Made of paper?' asked Caroline.

'Naturally,' said the little man. 'And you must cut it out. With a big ballroom and two kitchens with stoves and a broad staircase to the upper rooms and turrets with flags and battlements and parapets and a double front door with a flight of steps. And you must make footmen too, and cooks and dancing girls. Lots of dancing girls, because it's going to be a big party.'

Caroline had to laugh about it next morning, and yet she could not forget her dream. 'You know,' she thought, 'I'm really going to make it. A whole palace. For my own pleasure.'

She began to snip and stick and stick and snip. Walls with windows in them, turrets with battlements, the ballroom floor, the steps leading upwards.

'What are you making, Caroline?' her mother asked.

'Oh, a palace.'

By evening she had stuck two walls together and part of the stairs.

That night she dreamed of the little man again. He tripped across the ballroom and gave the walls a push which made the paper crackle. 'Is it really sturdy enough?' he asked.

'Yes, of course,' said Caroline.

'And where are the kitchens?'

'I've still got to do them,' said Caroline.

She made the kitchens the next day and the upper rooms with the broad staircase leading up to them and the turrets with flags on them.

'You'll have to hurry up,' said the little man on the third night of her dream. 'You've only got one day left. What about the flight of steps? Where are the cooks and footmen and dancing girls? And one of the towers must be higher.'

Caroline began immediately after breakfast. She cut out twelve dancing girls and stuck them on one leg in a circle round the ballroom. She cut out seven cooks on two legs by the stoves in the kitchens. She stuck an extra bit on the tower and made the steps and two big trees for the outside.

'Marvellous, child. Marvellous,' said her mother. 'Shall I put it away now?'

'On the table,' whispered Caroline.

But that night Caroline did not dream. No, she woke up instead. A light was shining in the room, a strange white light. She turned her head and then she saw it. In the middle of the table her paper palace stood sparkling and glittering as if a thousand lamps were burning inside it. Music was

pouring from the windows and shadows were moving against the transparent paper walls – the shadows of people dancing.

'The party!' thought Caroline. She was longing to sit up, but her bad leg wouldn't let her.

Then the people in the palace started to sing and clap their hands and laugh and shout hooray and 'Long live the Queen!' and Caroline saw the shadows of skipping, swaying, leaping and whirling people dancing across the white walls.

Then she looked at the tall tower. There at the top stood the little man of her dream, on guard.

'Hallo!' Caroline called to him.

At that very moment everything fell dark and silent.

How strange, thought Caroline, and next morning she thought again: how strange. Of course it was only a dream, but it seemed just as real as if I were awake.

'I say, how strange,' her mother was saying, as she set the castle beside Caroline's bed. 'I didn't remember that you had put a little man on the tower as well.'

Caroline's eyes opened wide. 'It wasn't a dream,' she whispered.

'What do you mean?'

But Caroline didn't answer. She peered with one eye through the window into the ballroom. And there, in the middle of the dance floor, inside the ring of twelve dancing girls on one leg, stood another figure, in a wide cloak and with a crown on her head: the queen.

And when the neighbours said, 'You did cut out *that* one cleverly, she's so real it looks as if she were alive,' Caroline would say, 'I didn't make that one.'

But no one believed her.

Back-to-Front Day

Have you ever heard of Back-to-Front Day? It used to be celebrated once a year you know, just like Twelfth Night and Easter; but Back-to-Front Day isn't celebrated any more and that is a great shame, because on Back-to-Front Day the grown-ups had to go to school.

And the children?

They were the masters and mistresses; they were the policemen and bus conductors; they sat in the offices and telephoned to New York and Paris; they were firemen and drove through the streets with bells clanging; they were doctors and nurses and bakers and butchers and long-distance truck drivers.

'Stand in the corner, Mr Dryasdust!' said Marie. Marie

was six and she had a class of twenty-three men and fifteen women. They were making much too much noise and not paying attention.

'Quiet!' cried Marie. 'Mrs Oakapple, stop chattering. Mr Drumbody, sit up straight. Have you finished your sums yet?'

Granny was late for school. She got into bad trouble with Marie and as a punishment she was not allowed to draw.

Johnny was a policeman with his helmet balanced on his ears and his coat down to his knees and the bottoms of his trousers rolled up. He stalked down the street with huge strides and a stern expression on his face.

'Hm, hm, what does this mean?' he cried sharply. 'Why are you not at school?'

'Oh, Constable, I . . . I . . .' stammered the man, 'I had to run an errand.'

'Fiddlesticks!' said Johnny crossly. He took out his note-book and pencil. 'Name?' he inquired.

'Mr Croop.'

'Quite so,' said Johnny. He wrote it down neatly, with two *o*s and then he blew his whistle and at once a police car with a blue flashing light appeared, driven by his friend Ernie.

'I have a truant here,' said Constable Johnny. 'Drive him straight to school.'

Mr Croop was pushed into the car.

'You haven't heard the last of this,' said Johnny.

He walked on and the next thing he saw was a brazen-faced woman coming out of a shop, as if she could do exactly as she pleased.

'Well, well, well, what's the meaning of this?' cried Johnny again.

'Not understand,' said the woman. She was a foreigner, a tourist who didn't know anything about Back-to-Front Day.

'Oh,' said Johnny. 'Get along with you, then.'

In the offices of the firm of Slosh and Splashing there was a tremendous bustle of activity.

Mandy was typing away on a typewriter with a red ribbon and Tommy was sitting behind the big desk which had at least four telephones on it, all ringing in turn.

'Hallo,' said Tommy. 'This is the director speaking . . . Yes, of course, twelve cases of paints. I'll get the driver to bring them along at once.'

And he dialled a number of another telephone: 'Hallo, Charlie, just take the truck and deliver twelve boxes of paints to Harry in the High Street.'

At the hospital two small doctors climbed on one bedside chair together in order to look down Mrs Allsebest-Ramble's throat, and Nurse Janice stuck a plaster on Grandpa Johnson's leg.

But the best part of Back-to-Front Day was the evening, because that was when the children put the grown-ups to bed. Very early. They told them a story, too – when the grown-ups had undressed obediently and cleaned their teeth and washed their hands.

'Don't forget your face, Daddy!' called Caroline.

Then the children went grandly downstairs to watch television, or go to the pictures, or drop in on Johnny and Errol and Sandra.

Very, very late at night came the last television news bulletin, read by Arthur and Leonie.

'Good evening, boys and girls! Back-to-Front Day has been celebrated today throughout the country. A mother in Birmingham refused to go to school and was arrested by three seven-year-old policemen.

'In Westminster the Chancellor of the Exchequer got

eight out of ten for arithmetic, but he earned himself a detention for singing.

'A severe outbreak of fire in the New Forest was put out by Fireman Gary.

'Her Majesty the Queen did not return to Buckingham Palace until a quarter past five. Her teacher had had to keep her in for an hour after school.

'That was the news. Good-byeee!'

With the familiar notes of the National Anthem, Back-to-Front Day came to an end.

It's a pity we don't celebrate Back-to-Front Day any more.

We hope you have enjoyed this book.
Some other Young Puffins are described
on the following pages.

SOME OTHER YOUNG PUFFINS

NINETY-NINE DRAGONS *Barbara Sleigh*

'I think sheep are soppy,' said Ben scornfully, so he
sent dragons over a gate to help him go to sleep
instead. But he hadn't intended the ninety-nine
greedy dragons to land in the same field as his
sister's fifty woolly sheep!

ADVENTURES OF SAM PIG
YOURS EVER, SAM PIG *Alison Uttley*

Two collections of magical and funny stores about
lovable, comical Sam Pig, Alison Uttley's
best-loved creation.

HALLO AURORA! *Anne-Cath. Vestly*

A sensitive and appealing book from Norway
about a family where Mother is the bread-winner
and Father – a student – stays home to look after
Aurora and the baby.

MARY KATE AND THE SCHOOL BUS
Helen Morgan

Mary Kate is five now, and more than ready for
school with all its grown-up new interests.

MAGIC AT MIDNIGHT *Phyllis Arkle*

Wild Duck had stood motionless on his inn sign
for 200 years or more, but the night he heard of
the midnight magic he stiffly flapped his wings
and came down to try the world.

WHERE MATTHEW LIVES *Teresa Verscoyle*

Happy stories about a little boy exploring his new
home, a cottage tucked away by the sea.

THE SHRINKING OF TREEHORN
  Florence Parry Heide

'Nobody shrinks,' declared Treehorn's father, but
Treehorn *was* shrinking, and it wasn't long before
even the unshakeable adults had to admit it.

BAD BOYS ed. *Eileen Colwell*
Twelve splendid stories about naughty boys, by
favourite authors.

A GIFT FROM WINKLESEA *Helena Cresswell*

Dan and Mary buy a beautiful stone like an egg
as a present for their mother – and then it hatches
out, into the oddest animal they ever saw.

GONE IS GONE *Wanda Gag*

Farmer Fritzl thought his wife's job of keeping
house was easy, so he stayed home to try it. But
the bad dog, the naughty baby and the cow that
fell off the roof soon made him change his mind.

TALES OF JOE AND TIMOTHY

JOE AND TIMOTHY TOGETHER *Dorothy Edwards*

Friendly, interesting stories about two small boys living in different flats in a tall, tall house, and the good times they have together.

THE BUS UNDER THE LEAVES *Margaret Mahy*

Adam didn't even like David, until they began playing in the old bus that made such a wonderful hideout, and soon they were the best of friends.

BANDICOOT AND HIS FRIENDS *Violet Philpott*

Lion promised his friends a surprise when he came home from India, but no one expected anything half as nice as friendly, funny, furry little Bandicoot, who was so kind and clever when any of his friends were in trouble.

UMBRELLA THURSDAY and A HELPING HAND
Janet McNeill

Good deeds sometimes have funny results, as the two little girls in these stories discover.

CANDY FLOSS AND IMPUNITY JANE
Rumer Godden

Two stories about dolls by an author who understands their feelings.

If you have enjoyed reading this book and would
like to know about others which we publish,
why not join the Puffin Club? You will be sent
the club magazine, *Puffin Post*, four times a year
and a smart badge and membership book. You
will also be able to enter all the competitions. For
details of cost and an application form, send a
stamped addressed envelope to:

The Puffin Club Dept A
Penguin Books Limited
Bath Road
Harmondsworth
Middlesex

and if you live in Australia, please write to:

The Australian Puffin Club
Penguin Books Australia Ltd
P.O. Box 257
Ringwood
Victoria 3134